KURT VONNEGUT

SEVEN STORIES PRESS

New York • London • Toronto

Copyright © 1999 by Kurt Vonnegut
Cover drawing © 1999 by Jules Feiffer
A Seven Stories First Edition

Seven Stories Press
140 Watts Street
New York, NY 10013

Distributed in Canada by Hushion House, Toronto.
Distributed in the U.K. by Turnaround, London.

Special thanks to Marty Goldensohn of WNYC, who served as city
desk editor to our roving reporter on the Afterlife, encouraging
him to keep digging away at the story, and getting public radio to
pay him a buck a word, which isn't bad for an out-of-the-way beat
like Heaven.

Portions of the introduction to this book were adapted from a
graduation address delivered by the author at Agnes Scott College,
Atlanta, Georgia, on May 15, 1999.

ISBN: 1-58322-020-8

Printed in the U.S.A.

9 8 7 6 5 4 3 2 1

contents

INTRODUCTION 7

GOD BLESS YOU, DR. KEVORKIAN *21*

INDEX OF PERSONS *79*

5

introduction

My first near-death experience was an accident, a botched anesthesia during a triple bypass. I had listened to several people on TV talk shows who had gone down the blue tunnel to the Pearly Gates, and even beyond the Pearly Gates, or so they said, and then come back to life again. But I certainly wouldn't have set out on such a risky expedition on purpose, without first having survived one, and then planned another in cooperation with Dr. Jack Kevorkian and the staff at the state-of-the-art lethal injection execution facility at Huntsville, Texas.

The following reports were recorded for later broadcast by radio station WNYC. I hope they convey a sense of immediacy. They were taped in the tiled Huntsville death chamber only five minutes or so after I was unstrapped from the gurney. The tape recorder, incidentally, like the gurney, was the property of the good people of Texas, and was ordinarily used to immortalize the last words of persons about to make a one-way, all-expenses-paid trip to Paradise.

There will be no more round trips for me, barring another accident. For the sake of my family, I am trying to reinstate my health and life insurance polices, if possible. But other journalists, and perhaps even tourists, will surely follow the safe two-way path to Eternity I pioneered. I beg them to be content, as I learned to be, with interviews they are able to conduct on the hundred yards or so of vacant lot between the far end of the blue tunnel and the Pearly Gates.

To go through the Pearly Gates, no matter how tempting the interviewee on the other side, as I myself discovered the hard way, is to run the risk that crotchety Saint Peter, depending on his mood, may never let you out again. Think of how heartbroken your friends and relatives would be if, by going through the Pearly Gates to talk to Napoleon, say, you in effect committed suicide.

———•—•——

About belief or lack of belief in an afterlife: Some of you may know that I am neither Christian nor Jewish nor Buddhist, nor a conventionally religious person of any sort.

I am a humanist, which means, in part, that I have tried to behave decently without any expectation of rewards or punishments after I'm dead. My German-American ancestors, the earliest of whom settled in our Middle West about the time of our Civil War, called themselves "Freethinkers," which is the same sort of thing. My great grandfather Clemens Vonnegut wrote, for example, "If what Jesus said was good, what can it matter whether he was God or not?"

I myself have written, "If it weren't for the message of mercy and pity in Jesus' Sermon on the Mount, I wouldn't want to be a human being. I would just as soon be a rattlesnake."

I am honorary president of the American Humanist Association, having succeeded the late, great, spectacularly prolific writer and scientist, Dr. Isaac Asimov in that essentially functionless capacity. At an A.H.A. memorial service for my predecessor I said, "Isaac is up in Heaven now." That was the funniest thing I could have said to an audience of humanists. It rolled them in the aisles. Mirth! Several minutes had to pass before something resembling solemnity could be restored.

I made that joke, of course, before my first near-death experience—the accidental one.

So when my own time comes to join the choir

invisible or whatever, God forbid, I hope someone will say, "He's up in Heaven now." Who really knows? I could have dreamed all this.

My epitaph in any case? "Everything was beautiful. Nothing hurt." I will have gotten off so light, whatever the heck it is that was going on.

———•———

Humanists, having received no credible information about any sort of God, are content to serve as well as they can, the only abstraction with which they have some familiarity: their communities. They don't have to join the A.H.A. to be one.

Yes, and this booklet of my conversations with the dead-and-buried was created in the hope that it would earn a little bit of money—not for me, but for the National Public Radio Station WNYC in downtown Manhattan. WNYC enhances the informed wit and wisdom of its community and mine. It does what no commercial radio or TV station can afford to do any more. WNYC satisfies the people's right to know—as contrasted with, as abject slaves of high-roller publicists and advertisers, keeping the public vacantly diverted and entertained.

Whereas formal religions surely comfort many members of the WNYC staff, that staff's collective effect on its community is humanism—an ideal so Earthbound and unmajestic that I never capitalize it. As I have used it here, "humanist" is nothing more supernatural than a handy synonym for "good citizenship and common decency."

———

I wish one and all long and happy lives, no matter what may become of them afterwards. Use sunscreen! Don't smoke cigarettes.

Cigars, however, are good for you. There is even a magazine celebrating their enjoyment, with male role models, athletes, actors, rich guys with trophy wives, on its covers. Why not the surgeon general? Cigars, of course, are made of trail mix, of crushed cashews and Granola and raisins, soaked in maple syrup and dried in the sun. Why not eat one tonight at bedtime?

Firearms are also good for you. Ask Charlton Heston, who once played Moses. Gunpowder has zero fat and zero cholesterol. That goes for dumdums, too. Ask your senator or senatrix or congressperson if guns, like cigars, aren't good for you.

———•———

My late Uncle Alex Vonnegut, my father's kid brother, a Harvard-educated life insurance agent in Indianapolis who was well read and wise, was a humanist like all the rest of the family. What Uncle Alex found particularly objectionable about human beings in general was that they so seldom noticed it when they were happy.

He himself did his best to acknowledge it when times were sweet. We could be drinking lemonade in the shade of an apple tree in the summertime, and Uncle Alex would interrupt the conversation to say, "If this isn't nice, what is?"

I myself say that out loud at times of easy, natural bliss: "If this isn't nice, what is?" Perhaps others can also make use of that heirloom from Uncle Alex. I find it really cheers me up to keep score out loud that way.

———•—•———

OK, now let's have some fun. Let's talk about sex. Let's talk about women. Freud said he didn't know what women wanted. I know what women want. They want a whole lot of people to talk to. What do they want to talk about? They want to talk about everything.

What do men want? They want a lot of pals, and they wish people wouldn't get so mad at them.

Why are so many people getting divorced today? It's because most of us don't have extended families anymore. It used to be that when a man and a woman got married, the bride got a lot more people to talk to about everything. The groom got a lot more pals to tell dumb jokes to.

A few Americans, but very few, still have extended families. The Navahos. The Kennedys.

But most of us, if we get married nowadays, are just one more person for the other person. The groom gets one more pal, but it's a woman. The woman gets one more person to talk to about everything, but it's a man.

When a couple has an argument, they may think it's about money or power or sex, or how to raise the kids, or whatever. What they're really saying to each other, though, without realizing it, is this:

"You are not enough people!"

I met a man in Nigeria one time, an Ibo who had six hundred relatives he knew quite well. His wife had just had a baby, the best possible news in any extended family.

They were going to take it to meet all its relatives, Ibos of all ages and sizes and shapes. It would even meet other babies, cousins not much older than it was. Everybody who was big enough and steady enough was going to get to hold it, cuddle it, gurgle to it, and say how pretty it was, or handsome.

Wouldn't you have loved to be that baby?

———

This rambling introduction is four times as long as the most efficient, effective piece of writing in the history of the English-speaking world, which was Abraham Lincoln's address on the battlefield at Gettysburg.

Lincoln was shot by a two-bit actor who was exercising his right bear arms. Like Isaac Asimov and Uncle Alex, Lincoln is up in Heaven now.

———•———

So this is Kurt Vonnegut, WNYC's now emeritus reporter on the afterlife, signing off on paper this time.

Ta ta and adios. Or, as Saint Peter said to me, with a sly wink, when I told him I was on my last round-trip to Paradise: "See you later, Alligator."

K. V.

November 8, 1998 and May 15, 1999

on my

near~death

experience

this morning, I found out what becomes of people who die while they're still babies. Finding that out was accidental, since I'd gone down the blue tunnel to interview Dr. Mary D. Ainsworth, who died last March 21, age eighty-five, in Charlottesville, Virginia. She was a retired but active-to-the-end developmental psychologist.

Dr. Ainsworth's extravagantly favorable obituary in the *New York Times* said she had done more research than anyone on the long-term effects of bonding between a mother and an infant during the first year of life—or, alternatively, the absentminded lack of bonding. She studied motherless babies in London, all kinds of mothering or lack of it in Uganda, and then here in the U.S. of A.

She concluded, with impressive scientific proofs, that infants need a secure attachment to a mother figure at the beginning of life, if they are to thrive. Otherwise, they will be forever anxious.

I wanted her to talk some about nature versus nurture, and also about the mothering I myself had received when a neonate—whether that might not go a long way toward explaining me.

But Dr. Ainsworth was bubbling over with excitement over how her theories were confirmed in Heaven. Never mind all the honors she'd received from fellow psychologists on Earth. It turns out that there are nurseries and nursery schools and kindergartens in Heaven for people who died when they were babies. Volunteer surrogate mothers, or sometimes the babies' actual mothers, if they're dead, bond like crazy with the little souls. Cuddle, cuddle, cuddle. Kiss, kiss, kiss. Don't cry, little baby. Your mommy loves you. Bet you have to burp. I'll bet that's the trouble. There. Feel better? Time to go sleepy-bye. Goo, goo, goo.

And the babies grow up to be angels. That's where angels come from!

This is Kurt Vonnegut, signing off in the lethal injection facility in Huntsville, Texas. Until the next time, goo goo goo and ta ta.

this morning,

thanks to

a controlled

near-death experience, I was lucky enough to meet, at the far end of the blue tunnel, a man named Salvatore Biagini. Last July 8th, Mr. Biagini, a retired construction worker, age seventy, suffered a fatal heart attack while rescuing his beloved schnauzer, Teddy, from an assault by an unrestrained pit bull named Chele, in Queens.

The pit bull, with no previous record of violence against man or beast, jumped a four-foot fence in order to have at Teddy. Mr. Biagini, an unarmed man with a history of heart trouble, grabbed him, allowing the schnauzer to run away. So the pit bull bit Mr.

Biagini in several places and then Mr. Biagini's heart quit beating, never to beat again.

I asked this heroic pet lover how it felt to have died for a schnauzer named Teddy. Salvador Biagini was philosophical. He said it sure as heck beat dying for absolutely nothing in the Viet Nam War.

after this

morning's

controlled

near-death experience I am almost literally heartbroken that there was no way for me to take a tape recorder down the blue tunnel to Heaven and back again. Never before had there been a New Orleans–style brass band, led by the late Louis Armstrong, to greet a new arrival with a rousing rendition of "When the Saints Come Marching In." The recipient of this very rare and merry honor, accorded to only one in ten million newly dead people, I'm told, was an Australian Aborigine, with some white blood, named Birnum Birnum.

When white settlers came in the nineteenth century, the natives of Australia and nearby Tasmania had the simplest and most primitive cultures of any people then on Earth. They were regarded as vermin, with no more minds and souls than rats, say. They were shot; they were poisoned. Only in 1967, practically the day before yesterday, were the surviving Australian Aborigines granted citizenship, thanks to demonstrations led by Birnum Birnum. He was the first of his people to attend law school.

There were no survivors on Tasmania. I asked him for a sound bite about the Tasmanians to take back to WNYC. He said they were victims of the only completely successful genocide of which we know. Louis Armstrong broke into our conversation to say the Tasmanians were as gifted and intelligent as anybody, given good teachers. Two members of his current band, he said, were Tasmanians. One played clarinet; the other one played a mean gutbucket, or slide trombone.

This is Kurt Vonnegut, WNYC's reporter on the Afterlife, signing off.

today's

controlled

near-death

experience was a real honey! I interviewed John Brown—whose body lies a-moulderin' in the grave, but whose truth goes marchin' on. One hundred forty years ago, come October 2, he was hanged for treason against the United States of America. At the head of a force of only eighteen other anti-slavery fanatics, he captured the virtually unguarded Federal Armory at Harper's Ferry, Virginia. His plan? To pass out weapons to slaves, so they could overthrow their masters. Suicide.

Law-abiding citizens opened fire from all sides, killing eight of his men, two of them his sons. He himself was taken prisoner by a force of United States Marines, sworn to uphold the Constitution. Their commander was Colonel Robert E. Lee.

John Brown wears a hangman's noose for a necktie up in Heaven. I asked him about it, and he said, "Where's yours? Where's yours?"

His eyes were like glowing coins. "Without shedding of blood," he said, "there is no remission of sin." It turns out that's in the New Testament, Hebrews 9:22.

I congratulated him on what he'd said on his way to be hanged before a gleeful, jeering throng of white folks. I quote: "This is a beautiful country." In only five words, he had somehow encapsulated the full horror of the most hideous legal atrocities committed by a civilized nation until the Holocaust.

"Slavery was legal under American law," he said. "The Holocaust was legal under German law," he said.

John Brown is a Connecticut Yankee, born in Torrington. He said there was a Virginian, Thomas

Jefferson, who had actually encapsulated God in only six words: "All men are created equal."

Brown was twenty when Jefferson died. "This perfect gentleman, sophisticated, scientific, wise," John Brown went on, "was able to write those incomparable sacred words while owning slaves. Tell me: Am I really the only person to realize that he, by his example, made our beautiful country an evil society from the very first, where subservience of persons of color to white people was deemed in perfect harmony with natural law?"

"I want to get this straight," I said. "Are you saying that Thomas Jefferson, possibly our country's most beloved founding father, after George Washington, was an evil man?"

"Let that, while my body lies a-molderin' in the grave," said John Brown, "be my truth which goes marchin' on."

(Choral rendition of one stanza of "Battle Hymn of the Republic.")

This is Kurt Vonnegut, signing off in the lethal injection facility at Huntsville, Texas. Until the next time, ta ta.

during

yesterday's

controlled

near-death experience, I chatted just inside the Pearly Gates with Roberta Gorsuch Burke, married for seventy-two years back here on Earth to Admiral Arly A. Burke, Chief of Naval Operations from 1955 to 1961. He led the navy into the Nuclear Age.

She died last July at the age of ninety-eight. Admiral Burke, by then retired of course, died a year before that at the age of ninety-nine. They met on a blind date in 1919, when he was in his first year at the Naval Academy. On that date, she was a last minute substitute for her older sister. Fate.

They married four years later. If past performance

is any indication, they will surely stay married there at the far end of the blue tunnel throughout all eternity. She said to me, "Why fool around?" President Clinton told her at her husband's funeral, when she still had a year to live, "You have blessed America with your service and set an example not only for navy wives today, and to come, but for all Americans."

The simple epitaph Roberta Gorsuch Burke chose for her tombstone here on Earth: "A Sailor's Wife."

dr. jack

kevorkian

has again

unstrapped me from what has become my personal
gurney, here, in the lethal injection facility at
Huntsville, Texas. Jack has now supervised fifteen controlled near-death experiences for me. Hey, Jack, way
to go! On this morning's trip down the blue tunnel to
the pearly gates, Clarence Darrow, the great American
defense attorney, dead for sixty years now, came looking for me. He wanted WNYC's listeners to hear his
opinions of television cameras in courtrooms. "I wel-
come them," he said, if you can believe it. This man
with the reputation of a giant, comes from a rinky dink
little farm town in Ohio.

"The presence of those cameras finally acknowledges," he said to me, "that justice systems anywhere, anytime, have never cared whether justice was achieved or not. Like Roman games, justice systems are ways for unjust governments—and there is no other sort of government—to be enormously entertaining with real lives at stake."

I thanked Mr. Darrow for having made American history much more humane than it would have been otherwise, with his eloquent defenses in court of early organizers of labor unions, of teachers of unpopular scientific truths, and for his vociferous contempt for racism, and for his loathing of the death penalty. And the late, great lawyer Clarence Darrow said only this to me: "I did my best to entertain."

Signing off now. Hey, Jack, waddaya say we go downtown for some of that good old Tex-Mex cuisine?

during

what has

been almost

a year of interviewing completely dead people, while only half dead myself, I asked Saint Peter again and again if I could meet a particular hero of mine. He is my fellow Hoosier, the late Eugene Victor Debs of Terre Haute, Indiana. He was five times the Socialist Party's candidate for president back when this country still had a strong Socialist Party.

And then, guess what, yesterday afternoon none other than Eugene Victor Debs, organizer and leader of the first successful strike against a major American industry, the railroads, was waiting for me at the far end of the blue tunnel. We hadn't met before. This great American died in 1926 at the age of seventy-one when I was only four years old.

I thanked him for words of his, which I quote again and again in lectures: "As long as there is a lower class, I am in it. As long as there is a criminal element, I am of it. As long as there is a soul in prison, I am not free."

He asked me how those words were received here on Earth in America nowadays. I said they were ridiculed. "People snicker and snort," I said. He asked what our fastest growing industry was. "The building of prisons," I said.

"What a shame," he said. And then he asked me how the Sermon on the Mount was going over these days. And then he spread his wings and flew away.

this is

kurt

vonnegut.

During my controlled near-death experience this morning, I had a continental breakfast with Harold Epstein, who died recently on his one-and-a-half-acre estate in Larchmont. He died of what can only be called natural causes, since he was ninety-four. This sweet man was a certified public accountant who, after a heart attack thirty-four years ago, surrendered in the company of his sweet wife Esta to what he himself called "Garden Insanity."

Esta is still among us, and I hope she's listening. These two love birds, Harold and Esta Epstein, traveled around the world four times, seeking, and often finding, wonderful new plants for American gardens, although neither one of them had any formal training as a horticulturist. At the time Harold's soul traded his old flesh for new flesh in Heaven, he was president emeritus of the American Rock Garden Society, the Greater New York Orchid Society, and the Northeast Region of the American Rhododendron Society.

I asked him for a WNYC sound bite I could use in summing up his life after his heart attack so long ago. He said, "My only regret is that everybody couldn't be as happy as we were." The late Harold Epstein said that the first thing he did after he got to Heaven, after picking a flower he'd never seen before, was to thank God for the priceless gift of garden insanity.

jack
kevorkian
and i thought

we knew all the risks I was taking during the controlled near-death experiences he has been giving me.
But today I fell in love with a dead woman! Her name
is Vivian Hallinan.

What made me want to meet her was one word in
the headline on her obituary in the *New York Times*:
"Vivian Hallinan, 88, Doyenne of Colorful West Coast
Family." What made someone or even a whole family
"colorful"? I had interviewed people in the Afterlife
who had been brilliant or influential or courageous or
charismatic or whatever. But what the heck was "col-

orful?" Two possible synonyms suggested themselves: "clownish" or "cute."

I have now cracked the code. "Colorful" in the *New York Times* means unbelievably good looking and personable and rich, but socialist.

You want to talk "colorful?" Vivian's late lawyer husband Vincent Hallinan, loaded with real estate bucks, back in 1952 ran for president of the whole United States on the Progressive ticket! How clownish and cute can you get, even in California?

Here's how clowning and cute. Vincent did six months in jail for his obstreperous defense of the labor leader Harry Bridges, who was accused of being a Communist during the McCarthy era. Vivian spent thirty days in the slammer for unladylike behavior during a civil rights demonstration in 1964.

And get a load of this: Her five sons were all in the demonstration with her, and one of them, Terrence, is now district attorney of San Francisco!

In Heaven, you can be any age you like. My own father is only nine. Vivian Hallinan has chosen to be eternally twenty-four, an utter knockout! I asked her how she felt about being called "colorful."

She said she would rather have been called what Franklin D. Roosevelt was called by his enemies: "A traitor to her class."

dr.

kevorkian

has just

unstrapped me from the gurney after yet another controlled near-death experience. I was lucky enough on
this trip to interview none other than the late Adolf
Hitler.

I was gratified to learn that he now feels remorse for
any actions of his, however indirectly, which might have
had anything to do with the violent deaths suffered by
thirty-five million people during World War II. He and
his mistress Eva Braun, of course, were among those
casualties, along with four million other Germans, six
million Jews, eighteen million citizens of the Soviet
Union, and so on.

"I paid my dues along with everybody else," he said.

It is his hope that a modest monument, possibly a stone cross, since he was a Christian, will be erected somewhere in his memory, possibly on the grounds of the United Nations headquarters in New York. It should be incised, he said, with his name and dates 1889–1945. Underneath should be a two-word sentence in German: "Entschuldigen Sie."

Roughly translated into English, this comes out, "I Beg Your Pardon," or "Excuse Me."

during today's

controlled

near-death

experience, I spoke to John Wesley Joyce, dead at sixty-five, former cop and minor league ball player, owner of the Lion's Head Bar in Greenwich Village from 1966 until it went bust in 1996. His was the country's most famous hangout for heavy-drinking, non-stop-talking writers in America. One wag described the clientele as "drinkers with writing problems."

The late Mr. Joyce said it was the writers who made it their club of their own accord, which hadn't pleased him all that much. He said he installed a juke box in the hopes it would interfere with their talking. But they kept coming. "They just had to talk a lot louder," he said.

WNYC's reporter on the Afterlife. During yesterday's controlled near-death experience, I had the pleasure of speaking with Frances Keane, a romance languages expert and writer of children's books, who died of cancer of the pancreas this past June 26 at the age of eighty-five. It seemed to me that her generally lauda-tory obit in the *New York Times* cut her off at the knees at the very end with this stark sentence: "Her three marriages ended in divorce." I asked her about this and she replied with shrugs and in three different romance languages.

"Así es la vida," she said.

"C'é la vita," she said.

"C'est la vie," she said.

And then: "Go fly a kite!"

during

my controlled

near-death

experiences, I've met Sir Isaac Newton, who died back in 1727, as often as I've met Saint Peter. They both hang out at the Heaven end of the blue tunnel of the Afterlife. Saint Peter is there because that's his job. Sir Isaac is there because of his insatiable curiosity about what the blue tunnel is, how the blue tunnel works.

It isn't enough for Newton that during his eighty-five years on Earth he invented calculus, codified and quantified the laws of gravity, motion, and optics, and designed the first reflecting telescope. He can't forgive himself for having left it to Darwin to come up with the theory of evolution, to Pasteur to come up with the germ theory, and to Albert Einstein to come up with relativity.

"I must have been deaf, dumb, and blind not to have come up with those myself," he said to me. "What could have been more obvious?"

My job is to interview dead people for WNYC, but the late Sir Isaac Newton interviewed me instead. He got to make only a single one-way trip down the tunnel. He wants to know what it seems to be made of, fabric or metal or wood or what. I tell him that it's made of whatever dreams are made of, which leaves him monumentally unsatisfied.

Saint Peter quoted Shakespeare to him: There are more things in Heaven and Earth, Horatio, than are dreamt of in your philosophy.

i have

just

interviewed

Peter Pellegrino, who died last March 26, age eighty-two, in his home in Newtown, Pennsylvania. Mr. Pellegrino was a founder of the Balloon Federation of America, and the first American to cross the Alps in a hot air balloon, and a validator of ballooning records for the National Aeronautic Association, and a balloon pilot examiner for the F.A.A.

He asked if I'd been a balloonist, and I said no. This was outside the Pearly Gates. I'm not allowed inside anymore. If I go inside again, Saint Peter says I'll be a keeper.

Saint Peter explained to Pellegrino that I wasn't

dead, that I was simply having a near-death experience, and would soon be back among the living.

When Pellegrino heard that, he said, "For God's
sake, man—get a tank of propane and a balloon while
you've still got time, or you'll never know what
Heaven is!"

Saint Peter protested. "Mr. Pellegrino," he said,
"this *is* Heaven!"

"The only reason you can say that," said Pellegrino,
"is because you've never crossed the Alps in a hot air
balloon!"

Saint Peter said to me, "Not only do you still have
time to go ballooning. You might also write a book
with the title, 'Heaven and Its Discontents.'" He said to
Pellegrino, ironically of course, "If you'd had crack
cocaine on Earth, I suppose Heaven would also be a
disappointment."

"Bingo!" said Pellegrino.

Even as a child, he said, he knew he belonged up in

the sky, not on the ground, and I quote: "...just as a fish flopping on a riverbank knows it belongs in the water." As soon as he was old enough, he went up in the sky at the controls of all sorts of airplanes, from World War I Jennies to commercial transports.

"But I felt like an invader, an alien up there, tearing up the sky with my propellers, dirtying it up with my noise and exhaust," he went on. "I didn't go up in a balloon until I was thirty-five. That was a dream come true. That was Heaven, and I was still alive.

"I became the sky."

This is Kurt Vonnegut, signing off with Jack Kevorkian in Hunstville State Prison. Until the next time, ta ta.

when

i went

looking

for James Earl Ray, confessed assassin of Martin Luther King, on today's controlled near-death experience, I didn't have to wander far and wide into Paradise. James Earl Ray died of liver failure on April 23 of 1998. According to Saint Peter, though, he has so far been unwilling to take a single step into the Life Everlasting awaiting him beyond the Pearly Gates.

He's no moron: he has an IQ of 108, well above average when measured against the intelligence of the general American population. He said to me that he wasn't going to set foot into eternity until a prison cell was built for him. He said the only way he could feel cozy forever was in a prison cell. In a cell, he said, he wouldn't give a darn how much time was passing by. Actually, he used the "s" word, wouldn't give a good "shit" how much time was passing by.

His conversation is still liberally spinkled with the "n" word for African-Americans, despite Saint Peter's pleas that he, for the love God, pipe the hell down. He said he never would have shot "the big n," meaning Dr. King, if he'd known the bullet would make what "the big n" said and fought for so effing famous all over the effing world. "Because of me," he said, "little white children are being taught that 'the big n' was some kind of American hero, like George effing Washington. Because of my little old bullet," he said, "the shit 'the big n' said has been carved into marble monuments and inlaid with effing gold, I hear."

This is Kurt Vonnegut in the effing state-of-the-art lethal injection facility in Huntsville, effing, Texas signing off.

during my

most recent

controlled

near-death experience, I got to interview William Shakespeare. We did not hit it off. He said the dialect I spoke was the ugliest English he had ever heard, "fit to split the ears of groundlings." He asked if it had a name, and I said, "Indianapolis."

I congratulated him on all the Oscars the movie *Shakespeare in Love* had won, since it had his play *Romeo and Juliet* as its centerpiece.

He said of the Oscars, and of the movie itself, "A tale told by an idiot, full of sound and fury, signifying nothing."

I asked him point-blank if he had written all the

plays and poems for which he'd been given credit. "That which we call a rose by any other name would smell as sweet," he said. "Ask Saint Peter!" Which I would do.

I asked him if he had love affairs with men as well as women, knowing how eager my WNYC audience was to have this matter settled. His answer, however, celebrated affection between animals of any sort:

"We were as twinn'd lambs that did frisk in the sun, and bleat the one at the other: what we chang'd was innocence for innocence." By *changed* he meant *exchanged*: "What we exchanged was innocence for innocence." That has to be the softest core pornography I ever heard.

And he was through with me. In effect, he told your reporter to go screw himself. "Get thee to a nunnery!" he said, and off he went.

I felt like such a fool as I made my way back to the blue tunnel. An enchanting answer to any question I might have asked the greatest writer who ever lived could be found in *Bartlett's Familiar Quotations*. The beaut about exchanging innocence for innocence was from *The Winter's Tale*.

I at least remembered to ask Saint Peter if Shakespeare had written Shakespeare. He told me that nobody arriving in Heaven, and there was no Hell, had claimed authorship for any of it. Saint Peter added, "Nobody, that is, who was willing to submit to my lie-detector test."

This is your tongue-tied, humiliated, self-loathing, semi-literate Hoosier hack Kurt Vonnegut, signing off with this question for today: "To be or not to be?"

never before

have i been

a tease

about a dead person I've interviewed, but now is the
time. Let's see how smart you are about the history of
big ideas.

For starters: This former Earthling, although not
quite twenty, published an idea as persistent in the
minds of thinking people today as Pasteur's germ
theory, say, or Darwin's theory of evolution, or
Malthus's dread of overpopulation.

Hint number two: Breeding will tell. This incredi-
bly precocious writer's mother was a famous writer,
too. Some of her books were illustrated by none other
than William Blake! Imagine having one's book illus-

trated by William Blake! Her most passionate subject: the right of women to be treated as the equals of men.

My mystery dead person's father was a writer, too, an anti-Calvinist preacher who wrote, most memorably, "God himself has no right to be a tyrant."

Who were the friends of such distinguished parents? William Blake and Thomas Paine, and William Wordsworth to name a few.

Hint number three: This person was married to a celebrity, as famous for the romantic disorder of his life as for his poetry. He inspired the suicide of his first wife, for example. As Romantically as you please, he drowned when he was only thirty.

Give up? I spoke in Heaven today to Mary Wollstonecraft Shelley, author, again before she was twenty, of the most prescient and influential science fiction novel of all times: *Frankenstein: Or the Modern Prometheus*. That was in 1818, a full century before the end of the First World War—with its Frankensteinian inventions of posion gas, tanks and airplanes, flame throwers and land mines, and barbed-wire entanglements everywhere.

I hoped to get Mary Shelley's opinions of the atomic bombs we dropped on the unarmed men, women, and children of Hiroshima and Nagasaki—and promise to try again. This time, though, she would only rhapsodize about her parents, who were, of course, William and Mary Wollstonecraft Godwin, and about her husband, Percy Bysshe Shelley, and his friends and hers, John Keats and Lord Byron.

I said many ignorant people nowadays thought "Frankenstein" was the name of the monster, and not of the scientist who created him.

She said, "That's not so ignorant after all. There are two monsters in my story, not one. And one of them, the scientist, is indeed named Frankenstein."

This is Kurt Vonnegut in Huntsville, Texas, signing off.

i have

returned

from heaven,

having interviewed the poet Dr. Philip Strax, S-T-R-A-X. He died at the age of ninety on the same day as the baseball player Joe Dimaggio, and was the author of this charming couplet:

> Tis better to have love and lust
> Than let our apparatus rust.

Author of three volumes of poetry, Philip Strax was also a radiologist. He refined the use of x-rays, previously useful mainly for looking at bones, so they could detect malignancies in the soft tissue of breasts. The number of women's lives extended by early detection of cancers, thanks to mammograms, in baseball terms might be called thousands upon thousands of R.B.I., or runs batted in.

The turning point in his career as a physician, if not as a poet, was the death of his beloved wife Gertrude at the age of only thirty-nine. She was killed by breast cancer detected too late. Every moment of his professional life thereafter was devoted to fighting that disease: What a success!

I found him at the edge of a crowd of frenzied angels who wanted their feathers autographed by Dimaggio. I said that his glowing obituary in the *New York Times* indicated that he was extraordinarily fond of women, and they of him. He recited these unabashedly feminist lines of his own composition:

> *Let us remind our poor men folk in deed and song:*
> *There are two types of men in this womanly world:*
> *Those who know they are weak,*
> *Those who think they are strong.*

This is Kurt Vonnegut, in the indispensable company of Jack Kevorkian, who has saved my life a hundred times now, signing off until the next time. Ta ta.

it is

late in the

afternoon

of February 3, 1998. I have just been unstrapped from a gurney following another controlled near-death experience in this busy execution chamber in Huntsville, Texas.

For the first time in my career, I was actually on the heels of a celebrity as I made my way down the blue tunnel to Paradise. She was Carla Faye Tucker, the born again murderer of two strangers with a pick-axe. Carla Faye was completely killed here, by the State of Texas, shortly after lunch time.

Two hours later, on another gurney, I myself was made only three-quarters dead. I caught up with Carla

Faye in the tunnel, about a hundred fifty yards from the far end, near the Pearly Gates. Since she was dragging her feet, I hastened to assure her that there was no Hell waiting for her, no Hell waiting for anyone. She said that was too bad because she would be glad to go to Hell if only she could take the governor of Texas with her. "He's a murderer, too," said Carla Faye. "He murdered me."

Dr. Jack Kevorkian supervises my trip to near death and back. Your reporter from the Afterlife has to sign off now. Jack and I have been asked to vacate the lethal injection facility, which must be prepared for yet another total execution. Speaking for both of us, I now say, ta-ta.

unfortunately,

the recent

legal difficulties

of Jack Kevorkian in Michigan, which is to say his con-
viction for murder one, have brought what I hope is a
temporary halt to the near-death experiences he has
been giving me. In order to provide some filler
between WNYC's appeals for money, I have interviewed a person who is still alive.

He is science-fiction writer Kilgore Trout. I asked
him how he felt about what happened in Kosovo,
Serbia. I tape-recorded his reply, but his upper plate
came unstuck again and again. For the sake of clarity, I
repeat in my own voice what he said.

And I quote:

NATO should have resisted the nearly irresistable tempta-
tion to be entertainers on television, to compete with movies
by blowing up bridges and police stations and factories and so
on. The infrastructure of the Serb tyranny should have been
left unharmed in order to support justice and sanity, should
they return. All cities and even little towns are world assets.
For NATO to make one unliveable is to cut off its nose to spite
its face, so to speak.

Show business!

The homicidal paranoia and schizophrenia of ethnic
cleansing does its worst quickly now, almost instantly, like a
tidal wave or volcano or earthquake—in Rwanda and now
Kosovo, and who knows where else? The disease used to take
years. One thinks of the Europeans killing off the Aborigines
in the Western Hemisphere, and in Australia and Tasmania,
and the Turks' elimination of Armenians from their midst—
of course the Holocaust, which ground on and on from 1933
to 1945. The Tasmanian genocide, incidentally, is the only

one of which I've heard which was one-hundred-percent successful. Nobody on the face of the Earth has a native Tasmanian as a forebear!

As is now the case with *Mycobacterium tuberculosis*, there is a new strain of the ethnic-cleansing bacterium that makes conceivable remedies of the past seem pathetic or even absurd. In every case nowadays: Too late! The victims are practically all dead or homeless by the time they are first mentioned on the six o'clock news.

All that good people can do about the disease of ethnic cleansing, now always a fait accompli, is to rescue the survivors. And watch out for Christians!

This is Kurt Vonnegut, signing off.

my career

in post-mortem

journalism,

dear listeners, almost certainly ends today. No soon-
er had Jack Kervorkian unstrapped me from my gurney, and I sat up and prepared to tell of my interview
in Heaven with the late Isaac Asimov, than Jack was
hustled out of here in handcuffs—to answer a murder charge in Michigan. Irony of ironies! This pur-
ported murderer has saved my life more than a dozen
times! With Jack gone, this lethal-injection facility no
longer feels like a home away from home to me.

Forgive my mixed emotions, then, as I mourn the
misery of one friend, Jack, who is still alive, while
rejoicing in the relative well-being of another—Isaac

Asimov, who died of kidney and heart failure, age seventy-two, eight years ago.

When on Earth, Isaac, my predecessor as honorary president of the American Humanist Association, was the most prolific American writer of books who ever lived. He wrote nearly five hundred of the things—to my measly twenty so far, or to Honoré de Balzac's eighty-five. Sometimes Isaac wrote ten published volumes in a single year! These weren't only prize-winning science-fiction. Many were scholarly popularizations of Shakespeare and biochemistry and ancient Greek history, and the Bible and relativity, and on and on.

Isaac has a Ph.D. in chemistry from Columbia, and was born in Smolensk, in the former Soviet Union, but was raised in Brooklyn. He hated flying, and never read Hemingway or Fitzgerald or Joyce or Kafka, according to his obituary in the *New York Times*. "I am a stranger," he once wrote, "to twentieth-century fiction and poetry."

"Isaac," I said, "you should be in the *Guinness Book of Records*."

And he said, "To be immortalized along with a rooster named 'Weirdo,' who weighed twenty-two pounds and killed two cats?"

I asked him if he was still writing, and he said, "All the time! If I couldn't write all the time, this would be hell for me. Earth would have been a hell for me if I couldn't write all the time. Hell itself would be bearable for me, as long as I could write all the time."

"Thank goodness there is no Hell," I said.

"Enjoyed talking to you," he said, "but I have to get back to work now—on a six-volume set about cockamamie Earthling beliefs in an Afterlife."

"I myself would cheerfully settle for sleep," I said.

"Spoken as a true humanist," he said, becoming more antsy by the second.

"One last question," I begged. "To what do you attribute your incredible productivity?"

Isaac Asimov replied with but a single word: "Escape." And then he appended a famous statement by the similarly prolific French writer Jean-Paul Sartre: "Hell is other people."

THE END

index of persons

Dr. Mary D. Ainsworth 21

Salvatore Biagini. 25

Birnum Birnum 27

John Brown. 29

Gorsuch Burke 33

Clarence Darrow 35

Eugene Victor Debs 37

Harold Epstein. 39

Vivian Hallinan 41

Adolf Hitler 45

John Wesley Joyce 47

Frances Keane 49

Sir Isaac Newton 51

Peter Pellegrino 53

James Earl Ray. 57

William Shakespeare 59

Mary Wollstonecraft Shelley 63

Dr. Philip Strax 67

Karla Faye Tucker 69

Kilgore Trout. 71

Isaac Asimov 75